MOTHER GOOSE

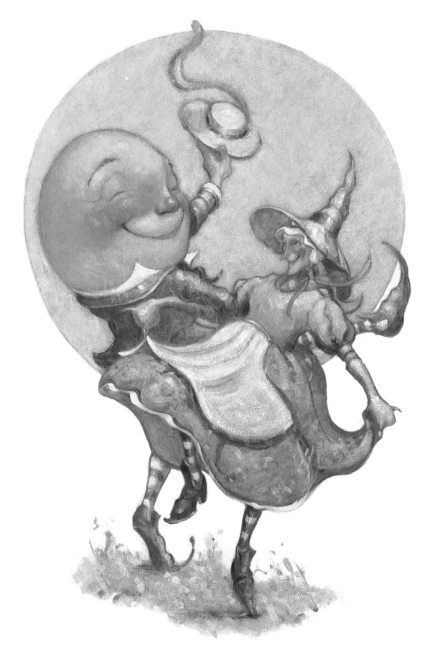

Selected & illustrated by Scott Cook

AN APPLE SOUP BOOK

An Imprint of Alfred A. Knopf • New York

To my nephew Christopher Boyd

APPLE SOUP IS A TRADEMARK OF ALFRED A. KNOPF, INC.

Copyright © 1994 by Scott Cook
All rights reserved under International and Pan-American Copyright Conventions. Published in the
United States of America by Alfred A. Knopf, Inc., New York, and simultaneously in Canada by
Random House of Canada Limited, Toronto. Distributed by Random House, Inc., New York.
Book design by Edward Miller.

Library of Congress Cataloging-in-Publication Data

Cook, Scott.
Mother Goose / selected and illustrated by Scott Cook.
p.   cm.
"An Apple Soup Book"
Summary: An illustrated collection of Mother Goose nursery rhymes, including well-known ones
such as "Old King Cole" and less familiar ones such as "Three Young Rats."
ISBN 0-679-80949-X (trade) — ISBN 0-679-90949-4 (lib. bdg.)
1. Nursery rhymes. 2. Children's poetry. [1. Nursery rhymes.]
I. Title
PZ8.3.C7695 Mo   1994
398.8—dc20   92-18296

Manufactured in the United States of America
10 9 8 7 6 5 4 3 2 1

CONTENTS

Old Mother Goose,
When she wanted to wander,
Would ride through the air
On a very fine gander.

And Old Mother Goose
The goose saddled soon,
And mounting its back,
Flew up to the moon.

Jack be nimble,
Jack be quick,
Jack jump over
The candlestick.

Pease porridge hot,
Pease porridge cold,
Pease porridge in the pot
Nine days old.

Some like it hot,
Some like it cold,
Some like it in the pot
Nine days old.

Old King Cole
Was a merry old soul,
And a merry old soul was he;
He called for his pipe,
And he called for his bowl,
And he called for his fiddlers three.

Now every fiddler, he had a fiddle,
And a very fine fiddle had he;
Twee tweedle dee, tweedle dee, went the fiddlers.
Oh, there's none so rare
As can compare
With King Cole and his fiddlers three.

Little Miss Muffet
She sat on a tuffet,
Eating of curds and whey;
There came a great spider,
Who sat down beside her,
And frightened Miss Muffet away.

Two make it,
Two bake it,
Two break it.

Jack Sprat could eat no fat,
His wife could eat no lean,
And so betwixt them both, you see,
They licked the platter clean.

Jerry Hall,
He is so small,
A rat could eat him,
Hat and all.

Baa, baa, black sheep,
Have you any wool?
Yes, sir, yes, sir,
Three bags full.
One for the master,
And one for the dame,
And one for the little boy
Who lives down the lane.

I bought a dozen new-laid eggs
Of good old farmer Dickens;
I hobbled home upon two legs
And found them full of chickens.

Donkey, donkey, old and gray,
Open your mouth and gently bray;
Lift your ears and blow your horn,
To wake the world this sleepy morn.

Come dance a jig
To my Granny's pig,
With a rawdy, rowdy, dowdy;
Come dance a jig
To my Granny's pig,
And pussy-cat shall crowdy.

Elsie Marley has grown so fine,
She won't get up to serve the swine,
But lies in bed till eight or nine,
And surely she does take her time.

Tom, he was a piper's son,
He learned to play when he was young,
And all the tune that he could play
Was "Over the hills and far away";
Over the hills and a great way off,
The wind shall blow my top-knot off.
Tom with his pipe made such a noise
That he pleased both the girls and boys,
And they stopped to hear him play
"Over the hills and far away."

Little Bo-Peep has lost her sheep
And doesn't know where to find them;
Leave them alone, and they'll come home,
Bringing their tails behind them.

Little Bo-Peep fell fast asleep
And dreamed she heard them bleating;
But when she awoke, she found it a joke,
For they were still a-fleeting.

Then up she took her little crook,
Determined for to find them;
She found them indeed, but it made her heart bleed,
For they'd left their tails behind them.

It happened one day, as Bo-Peep did stray
Into a meadow hard by;
There she espied their tails side by side,
All hung on a tree to dry.

She heaved a sigh, and wiped her eye,
And over hillocks went rambling,
And tried what she could, as a shepherdess should,
To tack again each to its lambkin.

Little Robin Red-breast
Sat upon a rail;
Needle, naddle went his head,
Wiggle, waggle went his tail.

Little Boy Blue, come blow your horn,
The sheep's in the meadow, the cow's in the corn.
Where is the boy who looks after the sheep?
He's under a haystack, fast asleep.
Will you wake him? No, not I,
For if I do, he's sure to cry.

Three little kittens, they lost their mittens,
And they began to cry,
Oh, mother dear, we sadly fear
That we have lost our mittens.
What! Lost your mittens, you naughty kittens!
Then you shall have no pie.
Mee-ow, mee-ow, mee-ow.
No, you shall have no pie.

The three little kittens, they found their mittens,
And they began to cry,
Oh, mother dear, see here, see here,
Our mittens we have found.
Put on your mittens, you silly kittens,
And you shall have some pie.
Purr-r, purr-r, purr-r,
Oh, let us have some pie.

The three little kittens put on their mittens,
And soon ate up the pie;
Oh, mother dear, we greatly fear
That we have soiled our mittens.
What! Soiled your mittens, you naughty kittens!
Then they began to sigh,
Mee-ow, mee-ow, mee-ow,
Then they began to sigh.

The three little kittens, they washed their mittens,
And hung them out to dry;
Oh, mother dear, do you not hear
That we have washed our mittens!
What! Washed your mittens, you're good little kittens,
But I smell a rat close by.
Mee-ow, mee-ow, mee-ow,
We smell a rat close by.

Hey, diddle, diddle,
The cat and the fiddle,
The cow jumped over the moon;
The little dog laughed
To see such sport,
And the dish ran away with the spoon.

Jack and Jill went up the hill
To fetch a pail of water;
Jack fell down and broke his crown,
And Jill came tumbling after.

The man in the moon came tumbling down,
And asked his way to Norwich.
He went by the south
And burned his mouth
With eating hot pease porridge.

23

I'll sing you a song,
Though not very long,
Yet I think it as pretty as any;

Put your hand in your purse,
You'll never be worse,
And give the poor singer a penny.

Hark, hark, the dogs do bark,
Beggars are coming to town;
Some in rags, and some in tags,
And some in velvet gown.

If wishes were horses,
Beggars would ride;
If turnips were watches,
I'd wear one by my side.

Christmas is coming, the geese are getting fat,
Please to put a penny in an old man's hat;
If you haven't a penny, a ha'penny will do,
If you haven't got a ha'penny, God bless you.

Oh, do you know the muffin man,
The muffin man, the muffin man.
Oh, do you know the muffin man
That lives in Drury Lane?

Oh yes, I know the muffin man,
The muffin man, the muffin man.
Oh yes, I know the muffin man
That lives in Drury Lane.

To market, to market, to buy a fat pig,
Home again, home again, jiggety-jig;
To market, to market, to buy a fat hog,
Home again, home again, jiggety-jog.

Humpty-Dumpty sat on a wall,
Humpty-Dumpty had a great fall;
All the King's horses, and all the King's men,
Couldn't put Humpty-Dumpty together again.

There was a crooked man,
And he walked a crooked mile.
He found a crooked sixpence
Against a crooked stile;
He bought a crooked cat,
Which caught a crooked mouse,
And they all lived together
In a little crooked house.

Mary had a little lamb,
Its fleece was white as snow;
And everywhere that Mary went
The lamb was sure to go.

It followed her to school one day,
That was against the rule;
It made the children laugh and play
To see a lamb at school.

And so the teacher turned it out,
But still it lingered near,
And waited patiently about
Till Mary did appear.

Why does the lamb love Mary so?
The eager children cry;
Why, Mary loves the lamb, you know,
The teacher did reply.

Old Mother Hubbard
Went to the cupboard
To fetch her poor dog a bone;
But when she got there
The cupboard was bare,
And so the poor dog had none.

She went to the baker's
To buy him some bread;
But when she came back
The poor dog was dead.

She went to the joiner's
To buy him a coffin;
But when she came back
The poor dog was laughing.

She went to the fruiterer's
To buy him some fruit;
But when she came back
He was playing the flute.

She went to the hatter's
To buy him a hat;
But when she came back
He was feeding the cat.

She went to the barber's
To buy him a wig;
But when she came back
He was dancing a jig.

She took a clean dish
To get him some tripe;
But when she came back
He was smoking a pipe.

She went to the tailor's
To buy him a coat;
But when she came back
He was riding a goat.

She went to the cobbler's
To buy him some shoes;
But when she came back
He was reading the news.

She went to the seamstress
To buy him some linen;
But when she came back
The dog was a-spinning.

She went to the hosier's
To buy him some hose;
But when she came back
He was dressed in his clothes.

The dame made a curtsy,
The dog made a bow;
The dame said, Your servant,
The dog said, Bow-wow.

If you are a gentleman,
As I suppose you be;
You'll neither laugh nor smile
At the tickling of your knee.

Sing a song of sixpence,
A pocket full of rye;
Four and twenty blackbirds
Baked in a pie.

When the pie was opened,
The birds began to sing;
Was not that a dainty dish
To set before the king?

The king was in his counting house
Counting out his money;
The queen was in the parlor
Eating bread and honey.

The maid was in the garden
Hanging out the clothes;
There came a little blackbird,
And nipped off her nose.

Rub-a-dub-dub,
Three men in a tub;
And who do you think they be?
The butcher, the baker,
The candlestick-maker,
They all jumped out of a rotten potato;
Turn 'em out, knaves all three.

Nose, nose, jolly red nose,
And what gave thee that jolly red nose?
Nutmeg and ginger, cinnamon and cloves,
That's what gave me this jolly red nose.

Dickery, dickery, dare,
The pig flew up in the air;
The man in the brown soon brought him down,
Dickery, dickery, dare.

Wee Willie Winkie runs through the town,
Upstairs and downstairs in his nightgown,
Rapping at the window, crying through the lock,
Are the children all in bed, for now it's eight o'clock?

There was a rat, for want of stairs,
Went down a rope to say his prayers.

There was an old woman who lived in a shoe.
She had so many children,
She didn't know what to do.
She gave them some broth without any bread;
She whipped them all soundly and put them to bed.

Three young rats with black felt hats,
Three young ducks with white straw flats,

Three young dogs with curling tails,
Three young cats with demi-veils,

Went out to walk with two young pigs,
In satin vests and sorrel wigs.

But suddenly it chanced to rain
And so they all went home again.

Rain, rain, go away,
Come again another day.

It's raining, it's raining,
There's pepper in the box,
And all the little ladies
Are holding up their frocks.

It's raining, it's pouring,
The old man is snoring;
He went to bed
And bumped his head
And couldn't get up in the morning.

Rain, rain, go to Spain,
And never come back again.

Mary, Mary, quite contrary,
How does your garden grow?
With silver bells and cockleshells,
And pretty maids all in a row.

Flying-man, Flying-man,
Up in the sky,
Where are you going to,
Flying so high?

Over the mountains
And over the sea,
Flying-man, Flying-man,
Can't you take me?

41

There was an old soldier of Bister,
Went walking one day with his sister,
When a cow at a poke
Tossed her into an oak
Before the old gentleman missed her.

Bryan O'Lin had no breeches to wear,
So he bought him a sheepskin and made him a pair,
With the skinny side out and the woolly side in.
"Aha, that is warm!" said Bryan O'Lin.

Cobbler, cobbler, mend my shoe,
Yes, good master, that I'll do.
Stitch it up and stitch it down,
And then I'll give you half a crown.

Cobbler, cobbler, mend my shoe,
Get it done by half-past two;
Half-past two, it can't be done,
Get it done by half-past one.

Pat-a-cake, pat-a-cake, baker's man,
Bake me a cake as fast as you can.
Pat it and prick it, and mark it with B,
And put it in the oven for Baby and me.

I see the moon,
And the moon sees me,
And the moon sees somebody
I want to see.
God bless the moon,
And God bless me,
And God bless the somebody
I want to see.